From : Grandma Petroff
9/7/09 - Labor Day Weekend

Any inquiries in regards to this book should be addressed to :
Forever Young Publishers
P.O. Box 216
Niles, Michigan 49120
Fax: 269-683-7153

Visit us on the Web:
www.foreveryoungpublishers.com
e-mail: cheri@foreveryoungpublishers.com

First Edition
Printed and bound in Canada
Friesens of Altona, Manitoba

Publisher's Cataloging-in-Publication
(Provided by Quality Books, Inc.)

Hallwood, Cheri L.
Winter's first snowflake / author, Cheri L. Hallwood
; illustrator, Patricia M. Rose. -- 1st ed.
p. cm.
SUMMARY: A whimsical story in which the first
snowflake of winter anticipates what will happen on his
downward journey to the ground.
Audience: Ages 2-8.
LCCN 2005909350
ISBN 0-9774422-0-9

1. Winter--Juvenile fiction. 2. Snowflakes--Juvenile
fiction. [1. Winter--Fiction. 2. Snowflakes--Fiction.]
3. Stories in rhyme] I. Rose, Patricia M. II. Title.

PZ7.H16552Win 2006   [E]
                                      QBI06-600022

Enjoy the Magic of Winter.
Cheri L. Wallwood

A book from
Forever Young Publishers
for

_____

Winter's First Snowflake

Written by
Cheri L. Hallwood

Illustrated by
Patricia M. Rose

How impatiently I wait,
'til the moment's

JUST

right

to be Winter's First Snowflake

all fluffy and White!!

BUT

When will it happen

How will I know??

Will I start out small,

then just magically GROW?

Will the North Win

Carry me far, far away, or

Will my journey be done

by the end of the day?

Will I float through the clouds like a feather so light?

Will I soar toward the heavens

like an eagle in flight?

Will I sparkle like sugar as

rift through the night,

Or Melt into a raindrop

with the morning's first light?

Will I land in a meadow?

Will i land on a house??

Will I be seen by a kitten, or startle a shy Mouse?

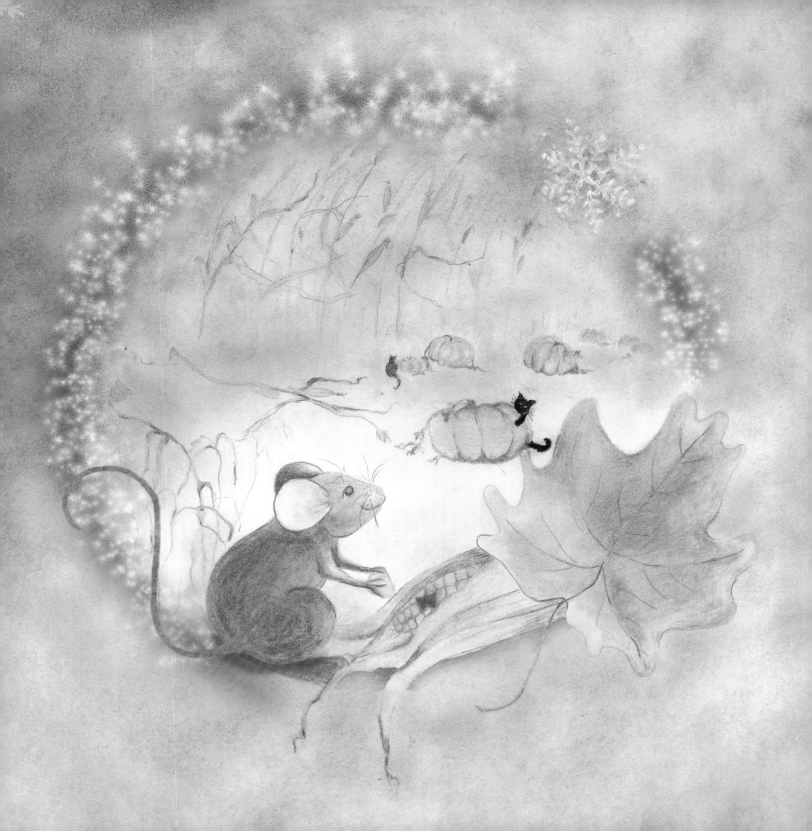

Or maybe* JUST MAYBE, I'll be part of a Smile***

as I land on the nose

of a Curious Child!

May EVERY snowflake of winter
bring you smiles, year after year,
as YOU impatiently wait
for the first snowflake to appear.